JIM COPP and Ed Brown, the creators of Playhouse Records, have long been popular with young listeners. *Martha Matilda O'Toole* is the first of their recorded songs to appear in book form.

Mr. Copp and Mr. Brown divide their time between California and Hawaii.

STEVEN KELLOGG, a graduate of the Rhode Island School of Design, has illustrated two books for children, *Gwot* and *Martha Matilda O'Toole*. His paintings and etchings have been exhibited in galleries in Washington, D.C. and New York.

Mr. Kellogg lives with his wife and children in Sandy Hook, Connecticut.

Martha Matilda O'Toole

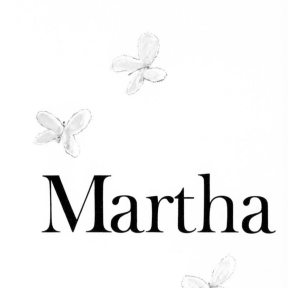

Martha

Bradbury Press / Englewood Cliffs, New Jersey

Matilda O'Toole

Story by **Jim Copp**

Pictures by Steven Kellogg

To our young listeners
—*Jim Copp and Ed Brown*
and to Kimberly
—*Steven Kellogg*

Martha Matilda O'Toole

Went skipping off to school . . .

But as she turned to go through the gate
Discovered that she had forgotten her slate.

Thought Martha, "The teacher won't like it a bit."
"I'd better go get it. My my!" And she did.

Martha Matilda O'Toole

Went skipping off to school . . .

But a cat in a willow tree hollered, "Hey look!
Martha Matilda's forgotten her book!"

First her slate,

Then her book,

Martha Matilda's forgotten her book.

Thought Martha, "The teacher won't like it a bit.
I'd better go get it. My, my!" And she did.

Martha Matilda O'Toole

Went skipping off to school . . .

But up by the corner she halted again,

Noticing now she'd forgotten her pen.

First her slate,
Then her book,
Then her pen,
Martha Matilda's forgotten her pen.

Thought Martha, "The teacher won't like it a bit.
I'd better go get it. My, my!" And she did.

Martha Matilda O'Toole

Went skipping off to school . . .

But a robin flew past her and said, "I got news!
Martha Matilda's forgotten her shoes!"

First her slate,
Then her book,
Then her pen,
Then her shoes,
Martha Matilda's forgotten her shoes.

Thought Martha, "The teacher won't like it a bit.
I'd better go get 'em. My, my!" And she did.

Martha Matilda O'Toole

Went skipping off to school . . .

But a boy on a bicycle yelled, "What a mess!
Martha Matilda's forgotten her dress!"

First her slate,
Then her book,
Then her pen,
Then her shoes,
Then her dress,
Martha Matilda's forgotten her dress.

Thought Martha, "The teacher won't like it a bit.
I'd better go get it. My, my!" And she did.

Martha Matilda O'Toole

Went skipping off to school . . .

But when she arrived, the teacher bowed low:
"The school is closed. It's Sunday, you know."

"If that is the case," said Martha, "I'll sit–
And wait until Monday. Oh, dear." And she did.

DATE DUE

MAY 1 4 1975

OC 06 '82

MY 27 '83

OCT 14 '88

MAY 19 '87 / APR 22 2003

MAY 06 2003

10-26-04 OCT 26 2004